Con

#28
$ 1.70

MY SUMMER BROTHER

MY SUMMER BROTHER

by
ILSE-MARGRET VOGEL

Illustrated by the Author

Harper & Row, Publishers

Library of Congress Cataloging in Publication Data
Vogel, Ilse-Margret.
My summer brother./ by. Ilse- Margaret
Vogel.— New York : Harper & Row, C1981.
SUMMARY: Nine-year-old Inge struggles to   86p. : ill.
understand the friendship between her mother and
the 20-year-old boy she herself is infatuated with.
[1. Friendship—Fiction] I. Title. 2. Mothers and Daughters
PZ7.V867Mw   [Fic]   80–7911   Fiction.
ISBN 0-06-026324-5
ISBN 0-06-026325-3 (lib. bdg.)

To Florence and Joe—
beloved friends
and patient listeners

CONTENTS

MY SUMMER BROTHER

🌿 Chapter One 🌿

"You are all I have," Mother said, hugging me. "My only one," and she pressed me so hard against herself it hurt. I loved my mother, but sometimes I could not stand her love for me. Especially after Erika, my twin sister, had died. I didn't like being snatched away from whatever I was doing to be hugged so hard.

At first, I could understand her grief. But now, six weeks after Erika's death, I began to wonder: Didn't Mother know I missed Erika just as much as she did?

She, at least, had other grown-ups to talk to. But I had nobody! Magda, the girl next door, was away a lot of the time; there were no other children in the neighborhood where we lived; and Dodo, my grand-mother, was visiting Uncle Max for the summer.

I wiggled myself out of Mother's arms.

"Don't you love me anymore?" she asked.

"Yes," I answered as I started to run away from her. Roland, our shepherd dog, jumped out of no-where and raced with me through the large garden to the row of fir trees at the end of our property. I looked back to make sure Mother hadn't followed us as I bent down to pick a marguerite to put behind my ear. Then I parted the branches of a large fir and slipped into my hiding place—a tent of tree trunks and branches that touched the ground. Breathless, I fell on the carpet of copper-colored pine needles, soft and fragrant from the warm summer day. Roland stretched out beside me, panting and licking my arm.

I lay on my back gazing up at the ceiling of my tent, where patches of light-blue sky shimmered through the dark green. Some of the branches hung over the iron fence and extended into the garden on the other side, a garden I did not really know. Only once when Erika was alive did we climb over the fence and investigate a small part of it. "We aren't doing anything wrong," we told each other. Nobody lived in that house and it was almost hidden by bushes and trees. But now I wished someone *would* live there. A family with ten children, all my own age. I turned to Roland and hugged him. "You are all I have," I whispered in his ear. Both his ears perked up and I laughed.

Suddenly Roland got to his feet, stretched his neck and listened attentively.

"There's nobody there, Roland," I said. "There isn't even a squirrel or a bird stirring. It's too hot!" But as soon as I said it, I heard a melodic whistle. It was a tune Mother often played on the piano, and as it got closer and closer, Roland started to bark. I tried to hush him up, but couldn't. Suddenly a face appeared over the bushes on the other side of the fence. It was a big, smiling face surrounded by curly blond hair. I jumped to my feet.

The bushes rustled and parted, and a tall young man pushed his right hand through the iron bars.

"Good day, princess," he said in a deep voice, "my name is Dieter." I had never heard that name before, nor a voice so deep. "Dieter," he repeated. "And what is yours, princess?"

"I'm not a princess" was all I could say, but I put

my hand in his. He smiled and said, "Well, a young lady with a flower in her golden hair and accompanied by a deer—oh, forgive me, it is a dog—*must* be a princess, I thought." Still holding my hand, he asked, "Don't you want to tell me your name?"

"Princess Inge," I blurted out. "Inge," I corrected myself, feeling confused.

"That's a nice name," Dieter said. "Inge." And the way he stretched the sound and made it linger in the air made me very happy. Dieter said he wanted to shake paws with my dog.

Roland let me raise his paw into Dieter's hand. "Roland," I said, "meet Dieter."

Roland sniffed Dieter through the fence. Dieter laughed and growled in a dog's voice, "I know you are curious about who I am and where I come from. Well, Roland, I come from the big city. My parents bought this house and we moved in this morning. We will be neighbors and friends—if you want to, that is," he added. While he spoke, Dieter had his eyes on me. "However," he continued, "until summer vacation starts, I will be away a lot. I have to go to the city every day to the art academy, you see." Dieter finished with a bark. Roland barked back and I laughed. "Any questions?" he asked Roland.

"Yes! How old are you?" popped out of my mouth.

4

"Let me see," Dieter said, "I'm not very good at arithmetic." He gave me a wink and started to count on his fingers. When he came to ten, he looked at me and said, "I guess that's how old you are?"

I nodded yes—and wished it were true. It was nice to be taken for older than my nine years. Dieter kept on counting. When he came to twenty, he stopped.

"Twenty!" I repeated, and could not hide the awe in my voice.

"Now you know a lot about me," Dieter said. "Tell me about yourself."

I didn't know what to tell him. How could I impress someone who was twenty? But when Dieter asked if I had any brothers and sisters, I knew I had something special to tell. "I have a *dead* sister," I said slowly, looking into his blue eyes. The smile left Dieter's face abruptly. To add more drama, I repeated, "A dead twin sister…and now I'm all alone."

Suddenly I felt so sorry for myself that tears filled my eyes. Dieter reached through the fence and stroked my hair.

"Don't cry," he said. His deep, soft voice was like a caress and made me wish for more, so I let the tears flow and leaned my head against the fence. Dieter stroked my hair. "You know what?" Dieter said after a while. "From now on you have a big brother. Would you like that, Inge-sister? Come, let's shake hands on that." But first he pushed a big white handkerchief through the fence. I wiped off my tears and we were just about to shake hands when I heard Mother's voice calling me. How awful! She *would* come just then and interrupt our pact of brotherhood. I put my finger to my lips and whispered, "My mother." But at that very moment there she was beside me.

"Your *mother?*" Dieter asked with great astonishment.

"Yes, I am Mrs. Sperl, Inge's mother," Mother said, smiling. "You must be our new neighbor. I saw the moving van from our upstairs window."

"Yes...yes, Madam," Dieter stammered and fell silent and just stared at Mother. Mother should have seen she wasn't welcome and left. But she didn't. She saw the big handkerchief in my hand and that my eyes were wet, and asked why I was crying.

"Erika," I murmured.

"You must forgive her," Mother said, putting her hand on my shoulder. "You see, just a few weeks ago—"

"Mother, I already told him everything!" I interrupted. "And he is my brother now. Aren't you, Dieter?"

I shook Mother's hand off my shoulder and

walked over closer to the fence, hoping Dieter would stroke my hair again. But he stood there silently, as if he couldn't speak at all.

"What is your name?" Mother asked. This brought Dieter to his senses. He apologized for not introducing himself, and politely answered the many questions Mother asked. It seemed as if their conversation would never end. Instead of listening, I tried to figure out a way to get rid of Mother. But when I heard *my* name, I listened again. Dieter was asking Mother if he could take me for a ride on his bicycle the following morning.

"No," Mother said, "that is not possible. Tomorrow is Sunday, and on Sunday mornings Inge's father, Inge and I always go for a walk."

"*Please*, Mother—" I begged, but she continued, "If you would like to join us, Dieter, you would be very welcome." Dieter nodded eagerly, and it was agreed he would meet us at ten the next day.

🌿 Chapter Two 🌿

That night I did not sleep well. In my evening prayer I had made many promises to God if only he would let the sun shine on Sunday. But my dreams were full of rainstorms, even snow. No Sunday walk. No Dieter! Yet when I woke, it was a lovely bright morning, and at ten Dieter arrived.

Papa greeted Dieter warmly. "Inge tells me she has a big brother now," he said.

"Yes, I'm a lucky fellow," Dieter said, putting his hand on my shoulder. "All my life I have wanted a little sister."

Mother came downstairs and we started out, taking the usual route through meadows and woods. I knew each bend of the path and every tree. But today everything seemed more beautiful to me. Whenever the conversation shut me out, Dieter would smile or wink at me, which made me feel better. They all talked about some man and whether he should become the next president of Germany. I didn't care who our next president would be, but they did and went on and on about him. At a hilly spot covered with birch and larch trees, Mother suggested we stop and rest. Papa spread out a blanket that he always carried in a knapsack on our walks, and he and Mother sat down.

"I don't want to rest," I said. "Come Dieter, I'll show you a pond on the other side of the hill."

"All right, Inge-sister," Dieter agreed.

We followed a brook lined with forget-me-nots. "Soon we'll come to a tree that has fallen across the brook," I told Dieter, "and we can cross over to the other side. I've done it many times."

But when we got there, the tree was gone. I sighed in disappointment. "Now we can't get to the pond," I said.

Dieter laughed. "We'll jump over the brook."

"It's much too wide," I said.

10

"Not for me," he said. "Watch!" Dieter took a few steps back, started to run and soared through the air, landing on the other bank of the brook. "You see?" he said, grinning.

I did not like being separated from him, but before I could say anything, Dieter was back beside me.

"Now I'll jump *with* you," he announced, picking me up. "Put your arms around my neck and hold on tight."

"Oh, Dieter, will it—" I was startled and a bit scared.

"Certainly it will work," he interrupted. "You are safe with me."

I closed my eyes and felt wonderful in Dieter's arms, but I did not feel safe till we both landed in the forget-me-nots on the other side. When we reached the pond, Dieter showed me how to skim stones over the surface of the water. His stones flipped straight across, bouncing off the water's surface a dozen times. Mine did not bounce, but sank after the first or second touch. Dieter said if I practiced I would learn, but I did not feel like practicing.

"Let's go back," I urged, looking forward to being in Dieter's arms again.

"All right," Dieter said, "but you stay here five minutes longer. I'll meet you at the brook."

I nodded, wondering what Dieter was up to. I threw a few more pebbles over the water, but they all sank. When I thought five minutes were up, I ran to the edge of the brook. Dieter stood there beaming. "Look, little sister," he said, "now you need not be afraid of the jump across. I have rolled some big stepping stones into the brook, so now you can walk across."

My heart sank.

"Something wrong?" Dieter asked.

"No, no," I answered, though I felt cheated out of being carried across by Dieter. I forced myself to smile and stepped swiftly over the stones to the other bank.

When we rejoined Papa and Mother, they were ready to go on. Our walk took us past a country inn, and as it was hot, we sat down in its shady garden and ordered cool drinks. My glass was the first to be empty.

"Won't you finish your drink?" Dieter asked me with a wink.

"But I did," I said.

"I will make a bet with you: There are still twenty drops in your glass," Dieter said.

I laughed. I could not believe it. But Dieter tore off a small piece of paper from a pad he carried in his pocket and put it to the rim of my empty glass. Then he tilted the glass as if he wanted to pour, and waited. A few seconds later a drop fell from the glass. Then a second, a third, a fourth—and on and on. The drops fell slowly, but they fell. We all laughed and counted till the twentieth drop dripped down into the saucer.

The day grew hotter and we walked home very slowly. Papa and Mother went ahead while Dieter and I followed hand in hand. "Do you know any other tricks?" I asked Dieter.

"I am *full* of tricks," Dieter replied. "Lots and lots of tricks. *And all for you!*"

At our garden gate we said good-bye to Dieter, and he went on down the road to his own house.

🌿 Chapter Three 🌿

Immediately after breakfast the following morning, I rushed to my hiding place. I knew Dieter would not be there; he still had two weeks of school. But I wanted to be in my secret place and think about him. I slipped through the branches and leaned my head against the fence, remembering Dieter's hand stroking my hair and how he had called me princess. I could hear his voice when I closed my eyes, and I kept them closed for a long time. When I opened them, I saw on the ground beside me a large rhubarb leaf with a mound of raspberries on it. One marguerite was stuck in the center.

"Oh, Dieter," I exclaimed. I knelt down and smelled the plump, ripe raspberries. I didn't want to eat them yet. They looked so pretty, and I wanted to show them to Mother first.

"Yes, they do look lovely" was all that Mother said, and she went back to the house.

I sat down and ate one raspberry. I didn't want to take the berries into the house, but went back to my hiding place two or three times every hour to eat a few. When they were all gone, I took the marguerite to my bedroom and put it in a glass of water.

As I stared at the pretty flower on my night table, I got an idea—I would make a thank-you card for Dieter. I worked on it all afternoon. I had to make the background dark enough for the white flower and the glass to show up clearly. It looked nice— but I didn't think it looked good enough for Dieter. I worked it over and over trying to improve it until I couldn't think of anything more to do. Then I wrote my thank-you note.

> *Thank you, dear Dieter.*
> *Raspberries are my favorite.*
> *You are too.   Inge*

The moment I wrote *raspberries*, I knew I should have put some raspberries in the picture. So I did. They made the picture look better and more complete.

I went back to my hiding place and tied the card to the fence with a ribbon. I hoped Dieter would find it that evening. Or the next day at the latest. But what if it rained at night? My card would be ruined. I listened to the weather forecast before going to bed; possibility of showers, the radio announcer said. I was already in my nightgown, but I slipped out of the house to fetch my picture. It was a dark and mild night. When I came near the garden's end, I was surprised to hear voices coming from my hiding place. It must be Papa and Mother, I thought; and since I did not want them to see me, I hurried back into the house. Halfway up the stairs I looked back and saw Papa talking on the telephone at the end of the hall. How did he get back in the house faster than I did, I wondered. I tiptoed to my room and got into bed. A short time later Mother stuck her head in the door to say good night. I pretended to be asleep.

It didn't rain that night, but my note to Dieter was still on the fence the next morning. It was also there in the afternoon and evening. It was gone the morning after, and in its place was a large envelope.

18

Don't bend was written on it in big letters. Carefully I opened the envelope and pulled out a stiff piece of drawing paper. I found a pencil drawing of myself smiling. Me! Almost life size! Dieter's signature was in the corner. There was also a note.

Good morning, Inge-sister. You draw very well. Thank you for your card. I am an artist too and I drew you from memory. But one day you must sit for me and I will make a pastel of you.

Your Dieter-brother

With Dieter's drawing in my hand, I ran to find Mother to show her my portrait. I finally found her in the gazebo. She sat, bent over, her hands covering her face. My footsteps on the wooden floor startled her and she lifted her head.

"You are *crying*, Mama," I said. She shook her head. I sat down beside her and rested my head on her shoulder. I could feel her whole body shake from sobbing. "It's Erika, isn't it?" I asked.

"It's not only Erika," Mother murmured, "it's Papa, too."

"Papa? Why Papa?"

"Yes," she said, "it's Papa." She sat up straight and dried her eyes. "Poor Papa has so much work, he has hardly any time for me. He often brings his work

19

home and he goes on working after dinner till midnight—or even later. Inge, I feel so lonely."

"But you have me, Mama. I am always here. I have time for you, and right now I have something special to show you." I put Dieter's drawing into her hands.

She studied it for a long time. "That's nice," she said at last.

"It's *great!*" I said with emphasis. "And you know what else? Dieter wants me to sit for him. For a pastel! He wrote me a note."

"Show me," said Mother.

I hesitated. "No, the letter is for me," I said and hid it behind my back.

"Well, would you want to sit still?" Mother asked. "Sit still for *hours?*"

"Of course I want to," I exclaimed, thinking of the hours I would spend with Dieter.

"Then let him know," said Mother, and she gave me a weak smile.

I wrote to Dieter that very morning.

You are a great artist. I WILL sit for you. When will you come to draw me? Tomorrow? What is your favorite color? Shall I wear my pink, my blue or my white dress?   Inge-sister

P. S. I have a red dress too.

20

I fastened my letter to the fence post and went back several times during the afternoon to see whether it was gone. Next morning there was a note from Dieter. "If it is all right with your mother, I will come over at four o'clock Saturday afternoon."

Saturday after lunch I went to my room to prepare myself for the sitting. Since Dieter had not let me know whether he wanted me in pink, blue, white or red, I found it difficult to decide what to wear. I must have changed dresses ten times by the time Dieter arrived. I still had to comb my hair and put the thin gold chain with the heart pendant around my neck. The golden heart could be opened to show two small photos. Sometimes I had Papa and Mother inside. Sometimes I took out Mother's photo and replaced it with Dodo's. But it was important to me always to know whom I was carrying with me. I opened it and saw Papa and Dodo. Good.

When I came downstairs, Dieter and Mother were sitting on the terrace on the white wicker bench. Mother was reading aloud to Dieter. They both raised their eyes when I appeared, but Mother kept on reading. Dieter moved closer to Mother to make room for me beside him. I wanted to say something, but Dieter hushed me up. Finally Mother put down the book and I jumped up.

"Where do you want me to sit?" I asked Dieter.

"Over there," said Mother, pointing to a chair at the other end of the terrace.

I went over and sat down, but Dieter did not follow me. Instead he had a long conversation with Mother about what she had just read to him. Words like "philosophy," "transfiguration" and "improvisation" were going back and forth between them. Words that had no meaning to me. Anger began to grow within me. Anger against the words and against Mother for reading that stuff to *my* Dieter. It was almost five o'clock and Papa would be home by six. Where were the long hours with Dieter I had hoped for?

"I am waiting," I shouted. Mother and Dieter turned their heads to me. Mother frowned. Dieter smiled.

"All right," he said, picking up his drawing pad and a large flat box filled with pastels. He pulled up a chair facing mine and sat down.

"Do you like my blue dress?" I asked.

"It's perfect," Dieter answered.

I turned my head to see what Mother was doing.

"You must hold still," Dieter said.

Mother remained on the bench reading her book. She should go to the kitchen and start preparing

supper, I thought. But she didn't.

"You don't look happy," Dieter said after a few minutes. "Would you rather *not* sit for me today?"

"No, no, I *want* to," I assured him.

It was easy to sit still and watch Dieter watch me. His eyes would linger on my face for a long time before he would lower them to the pad and draw. Time and again his long, searching look was followed by a few lines on the paper. I felt very close to him, as if I belonged to him. I wasn't even aware that Mother had left till suddenly I heard Papa's voice.

"Ah, young Leonardo at work." He put his hand on Dieter's shoulder. "Go on. Don't stop," he said. "But maybe you will let me kiss your sister just once?"

Dieter said he was ready to stop anyhow. "I don't want to tire my Mona Lisa. She might lose her lovely smile," he said.

I felt wonderful and very important. I knew who Mona Lisa was. A reproduction of the painting hung in Dodo's room. Now I wanted to go and study her smile and see how really lovely Dieter thought I could be.

"I have to go home now," Dieter said. "Please, Inge, say good-bye to your mother for me."

"Will you join us for our Sunday walk tomorrow?" Papa asked, and Dieter said he would like to.

24

I walked Dieter to the garden gate.

"Let's take our drawing pads and pencils tomorrow," Dieter suggested. "We might want to draw the landscape."

That was a wonderful idea, I thought.

*   *   *

Next day when Papa and Mother rested at the same spot they had rested a week ago, Dieter and I went to the pond to draw. Well—I really didn't know how to start. Dieter saw the trouble I was in and advised me to start with the big shapes—the pond, the horizon, the sky. Then fill in the smaller ones—the trees, bushes and rocks.

Dieter was finished long before I was, but he did not rush me. He showed me his landscape and I got discouraged, seeing so fine a drawing. But he assured me my drawing was fine, only different from his. Encouraged, I went on while he worked a bit more on his.

"We should go back now," Dieter said after a while. "I promised your father we wouldn't be more than an hour."

I showed Dieter my sketch. "It's not finished," I said apologetically.

"I finished mine," he said. "Look."

I burst out laughing. Dieter had added a mermaid

to the pond. And when I looked closer, the mermaid resembled me. Papa and Mother laughed too when we showed them Dieter's drawing.

Before we parted from Dieter, Papa asked him whether he would like to come over after lunch and work on my portrait. "My wife and I have to go out for a few hours, but I'm sure Inge will enjoy having you over."

"I will! I will!" I burst out, and Dieter promised to come.

🌿 Chapter Four 🌿

As soon as my parents left, I went to Dodo's room to study the Mona Lisa's smile. But it only confused me—one second she seemed to smile; the next, the smile was gone. As hard as I tried, I could not learn from her how to smile so mysteriously. There was no time anyhow, because I heard Roland bark a greeting to Dieter.

Dieter's hands were full. He carried his drawing pad, the box of pastels and two small baskets filled with raspberries.

"Oh, you've brought me *two* baskets of raspberries," I exclaimed with delight.

"No," Dieter said, "only *one* is for you. The other one is for your mother. Here, this is yours, the one with the marguerite."

We went to the terrace and I sat down. Dieter took my head between his hands and gently turned it to the same position as when he had started my portrait. Then he began to draw. I had expected the sittings to be filled with chatter and laughing, but hardly a word was spoken. Dieter's blue eyes studied my face, and when his eyes met mine, my heart beat faster. I had never seen Dieter so serious. But it was all right. I was floating in the air, and the air was filled with the humming of bees and the sweet scent of the honeysuckle vine climbing over the edge of the terrace. Once in a while a bird chirped in the nearby trees.

"Thank you, princess." Dieter's voice came from far away. "You have sat very quietly today. And for *such* a long time."

"A long time?" I asked, and Dieter laughed.

"Yes, for a whole hour."

"Let me see what you did."

Dieter handed me the pad. There was not much on it. Only my brown eyes, a suggestion of the nostrils and a faint oval line ending at the neck.

"I must go now," Dieter said. "I'm expecting a friend from the city." He closed the pastel box and put a piece of tissue paper over my faceless eyes.

I had hoped we would do something special after the sitting. But since Dieter had to leave, I walked him to the gate, talking loudly and laughing a lot so he would not see how sad I was.

Then I went back to the terrace and sat down. What was I going to do with the whole afternoon? Ah, the raspberries! I started to eat them slowly, one berry at a time, from Mother's basket. I wanted her to see how pretty mine looked with the marguerite. I finished the whole basketful. On the bottom was a lacy white paper, stained pink by raspberry juice. I took it out to throw it away, but under it was another piece of paper. As I unfolded it, I saw there was writing on one side, Dieter's handwriting. It was arranged like a poem, but I couldn't read it because it was written in a language I did not know. Once in a while the word "Margarete," my mother's name, appeared among the lines. Was the poem written to a Margarete? Or did Dieter write the poem for Mother? If only Dodo were home. She would know. I stared at the poem a long time, hoping something would reveal itself if I stared at it long enough. I tried to read it out loud, but nothing made sense, only "Margarete" and "Oh, Margarete."

My curiosity grew until I thought I was going to burst. I *had* to talk to someone! Emma, our housekeeper! Even if she didn't know what language it was, she might know something. But it was Sunday, and Emma's afternoon off. I had been told *never* to disturb Emma during her free time. But I couldn't hold myself back. I ran upstairs and knocked at her door.

"It's Inge," I announced.

"Come in, come in," Emma called. She was stretched out on her bed. The bed had red-and-white-checked linen on it. Why do we always sleep on *white* linen, I thought. Red and white checks are much nicer. I also liked the shape of her room: One wall was slanted and met the ceiling at a flat angle. The room was small but cozy. Photos with paper flowers stuck behind them were pinned all over the walls. Stockings and underwear hung over the back of a chair. Mother never allowed *me* to do that. On a table in a corner stood an old-fashioned phonograph with a huge fluted horn.

"Emma, you have a phonograph!" I exclaimed.

"Certainly," Emma said, yawning. "It's old, but it still plays. Just jumps a groove here and there." She

went over to the phonograph and cranked the handle. A blurred and hoarse voice began to moan about love and parting, heartbreak and hope.

"Isn't it nice?" Emma asked.

I nodded. When the voice became nothing but a scratchy sound, Emma filled in the words. And when the needle jumped a groove, Emma lifted it off the record and sang the missing lines to me.

When the song ended, Emma sighed and said, "Well, that beautiful record was a present from my second fiancé. Look, there is his photo on the wall. The one with the red carnation. And next to him, with the blue cornflower, that is my third fiancé. He was swell, believe me. But you know which one was the very best of all? My fourth." And she swayed her head from side to side and smiled.

"How many fiancés did you have?" I asked.

"Well, let me see," Emma said, "maybe six, maybe seven. I can't quite remember. Of course, I didn't have them all at the same time. I'm a nice girl and...I know a lot." She looked at me meaningfully.

"I guess you do," I said. "Maybe you know what this means?" I asked, pushing the poem in front of her.

Emma looked at it. She squinted her eyes and frowned. "That is foreign," she said, slightly disgusted, "and I don't care for foreign things."

"But it's just another language, Emma. It's as good as our language for the people who know it."

Emma shook her head. "Foreign is not good," she said with emphasis.

"But people write songs and poems in foreign languages, too," I insisted.

Emma could not be persuaded and repeated, "Foreign *is not good.*"

There was no hope. I had to give up.

"Where did you get it, anyhow?" Emma asked.

"Never mind," I said. "I just happen to have it."

Emma lost interest and changed the subject. "Is your portrait finished?" she asked.

"Of course not! It will be a masterpiece like the Mona Lisa, and that takes *time!*"

"I see," Emma said and stretched out on her bed again.

"I have to go now," I said, and left feeling even more dejected.

I decided to put the poem back under the lacy paper of the little basket and to put all the raspberries from my basket on top. I even added the marguerite, which Dieter had meant to be mine.

But an hour later I changed my mind. I didn't want Mother to have this poem. I took out all the raspberries, crunched the poem into a ball and buried it under a tree. The berries looked bad by now, squeezed and mashed from having been handled so much. So I decided to eat them and not say anything to Mother.

🌿 Chapter Five 🌿

Days passed without my seeing Dieter. Then one morning, just as I was about to give up hope of ever seeing him again, I found a small box with a magnifying glass inside by the fence in my hiding place. There was a note from Dieter.

Use this to look at tiny things: flower buds, ladybugs, seeds of grass and pebbles.

I spent hours looking at little things through the

magnifying glass, and found beauty where I had not expected it. Even a cherry pit I once would have spit carelessly on the ground looked interesting.

But a day came when nothing was interesting. It was hot and everybody was slow and listless. After lunch I went upstairs to Mother's bedroom. I had been told always to knock before opening the door, but this time I forgot. I found Mother sitting in front of her vanity table, smiling at herself in the mirror. Her back was to the door and she did not see me as she rolled a strand of hair around her curling iron. When she pulled it off, a lovely curl formed. She shook her head lightly, making the curl bounce, and smiled even more. She looked so pretty and young. I could hardly believe she was my mother, my mother who could scold so severely, who could be so stern and who, since Erika's death, was so sad most of the time. I stood quietly at the door, watching. Suddenly Mother got up and moved her face closer to the mirror. Her eyes wandered searchingly over her face while her left hand pulled down the neckline of her white blouse until it revealed as much of her bosom as showed on ladies in old paintings. I must have gasped, because Mother turned around and motioned me to her side. "Would *you* like a curl too?" she asked, still smiling. But it was a very different

smile from the one she had given herself a few seconds ago.

"Come on, tell me," Mother said.

"Tell you what?" I stammered.

"Whether you want a curl," she replied.

"I don't think so," I answered. "Not now. Maybe later."

"Later I won't be here," Mother said and took my hand. "Why are you trembling?"

"I'm not trembling," I said and withdrew my hand.

Mother sat down again and resumed curling her hair. I watched silently. "Oh, dear, it is so hot today," she said finally. And when I did not respond, she asked, "Aren't you hot?"

I was hot. Inside and out. But I shook my head. I did not feel like saying anything. I wanted to think about those two different smiles. One of them I knew. The other one was a mystery to me.

At last Mother was finished. "I have to go to the village," she said, stroking my head.

"Can I go with you?" I asked.

"I don't think so," she said. "It is much too hot. You can join me at six o'clock at the railroad station to meet Papa's train. All right?"

"Let me go with you now," I pleaded.

"No, no. It's much more comfortable here. I have a

few boring errands in the village. Stay here, darling."

We went downstairs and Mother left. The house was quiet except for the faraway voice of Emma singing her favorite song in the kitchen as she washed the luncheon dishes. The melody was slow and haunting, and Emma interrupted it frequently with moans and sighs. It had brought tears to my eyes the first time I had heard it. But the repetition of words like "forsaken," "lonely" and "loving," "longing" and "weeping" began to sound silly to me after a while.

I took a book from my shelf, but I couldn't concentrate. It's boring anyhow, I said to myself, kid stuff. Besides, I didn't really feel like reading. I went outdoors. The stones on the terrace felt hot through the thin soles of my sandals, so I went back into the coolness of the house.

The tall grandfather clock struck three. Three whole hours before I could go to the station. I sat down and watched the large brass pendulum of the clock swing back and forth. When Dodo was home, we sometimes sat together and watched this steady movement and enjoyed the melodious ticktock punctuating each swing. Then it was fun, but today the sound and the motion made me sad.

I decided to go to my hiding spot. I knew there was

little hope of meeting Dieter. He was probably still in school, I thought. So my surprise was great when I found two pairs of red cherries, each connected by their stems, hanging in the fence. "A pair of earrings for my Inge-sister" was written in red pencil on a tiny roll of paper. That's nice, I thought. Red is the color of love. It said so in Emma's songs. I pushed my hair behind my ears to hang the cherries over them and ran back inside the house.

Strange, I thought, the cherries were not at the fence when I went there this morning. Was Dieter home today? I walked up the stairs in a daze and into my parents' room to look at myself in Mother's vanity-table mirror. The cherries looked nice, but childish, I decided, so I ate them.

Then I pulled my hair from behind my ears and tried to smile the way Mother had smiled at herself. But my smile remained my everyday smile. I gave up and busied myself with the wonderful things on Mother's vanity table. They were all familiar to me, but I never tired of sniffing the strong scent of Mother's lily-of-the-valley perfume or of brushing my hair with her silver brush. From time to time I stopped and tried the special smile. In vain. Finally I opened the shiny black lacquer box, inlaid with mother-of-pearl, which held Mother's jewelry. I tried on one necklace, then another, then a bracelet, then two rings, which fit only on my thumbs. I had done this many times before, but today I had the urge to empty the box completely, down to its blue velvet bottom. I didn't stop there, because the velvet seemed to be loose. When I pulled, it lifted slowly on one side and I was surprised to discover a photo of Mother underneath.

Her face showed first, but it was not surrounded by the mass of hair that was usually piled up on her head. Instead, her long blond hair fell down over her shoulders, barely covering her breasts. I let the velvet drop over the photo and shut the lid. My impulse was to run away, but I sat motionless, staring at the box. I felt dizzy and could not think. Then, without really intending to, I opened the box again. I lifted up the velvet bottom to look at the photo again. I hoped I had seen wrong, that it was not a photo of Mother. But it was. Her eyes were cast down and there was a faint hint of the mysterious smile. On the bottom of the photo Papa had written: "To My Beloved Wife." I looked at the photo for a long time. "Oh, Mother," I said with a sigh, "I never want to see you like this again." I covered her with the blue velvet and buried her under her jewelry.

I sat there thinking about Mother. I thought of the

way she looked in the kitchen: an apron around her middle, a spoon in her hand, bent over a boiling pot on the stove. That was the way I knew and loved her. I also loved her when she sat at the piano and played the "Moonlight Sonata" with a faraway smile on her face. That was Mother! But the woman in the photo I did not know—and did not like.

I went downstairs and met Emma in the hall. "If you help me shell peas, I'll sing you a new song," she said.

We sat down at the kitchen table and Emma started her song. Again it was about longing and waiting, waiting in vain and in tears. But today it made sense to me. I thought of Dieter and how much I wanted to see him. It would be nice if he were here now when Mother was away. He could give *me* his full attention, which he couldn't when Mother was around. He was too polite for that. Emma sang her new song two times, and each time she came close to tears.

"It's beautiful, isn't it?" she said.

I nodded yes and kept on shelling peas.

"How come your boyfriend doesn't visit you?" Emma asked suddenly. "I saw him just before lunch."

"Well," I answered, trying to sound cheerful, "he

can't always be with me. You know he has to study. He is very bright."

"I know, you told me so before. But he could just come and say hello. He knows you are lonely with Dodo and Magda away for the summer."

"Don't worry," I said, "he left me a little present at our secret spot."

"Secret!" Emma laughed. "Big secret."

I got up. "I have to go to the station now to meet Papa," I declared.

"It's much too early," Emma said.

"Never mind. I have things to arrange."

"Arrange?" Emma laughed again. *"Arrange!"*

"It's very important," I said, trying to sound important.

I started for the railroad station half an hour early. I went out of my way to pass Dieter's house, but there was no sign of him. When I reached the station, I watched the express trains as they whizzed by without stopping. Suddenly I missed Erika very much. We often had gone to the station together to meet Father coming home from work. Now I was alone. Three minutes before Papa's train was due to pull in, there was still no sign of Mother.

The big hand of the station clock made another jump. Two minutes to the train. And just as it jumped again, Mother came rushing through the door, her face flushed, her hat tilted on her head. She clutched one red rose in her hand.

"I had to run the last part of the way," she explained, dabbing her face with her handkerchief. "My, how hot it is."

I didn't want to look at her and I didn't need to, because at that very moment Papa's train pulled into the station. When we saw him coming toward us, Mother pushed the red rose into my hand. "*You* give it to Papa," she said.

"Where did it come from?" I asked. "We have no red roses in our garden."

At that moment Papa joined us. He kissed Mother, then me, and asked, "Did you bring the rose for me, darling?"

I handed him the wilted rose without saying anything. It must have been without water for hours, I thought. We walked the short way home holding hands. I usually walked between Papa and Mother, but today I walked next to Papa on the outside. The heat had subsided and it was pleasant and warm. The birds, silent during the day, began singing again in the leaves of the chestnut trees over our heads. When we got home, Emma had a cold supper ready for us on the terrace, and while we ate, Papa told us about his day in town.

"It's too much work," he said. "I shouldn't complain that I have so many clients, I know, but just the same it is too much." He put his hand on Mother's. "I had promised to go to the Zobten Mountain for a week with the two of you, but I can't. A very important case has come up, and since I can't foresee its end, I want you two to go without me as we had planned."

"Oh, Papa," I said, "it won't be fun without you! You always find your way through woods and over hills and mountains. Mother and I will get lost without you."

"Yes, it won't be the same," Mother agreed. "We'll be lonely without you."

"I'm really sorry, Margarete," Papa said, and turning to me, he said, "Inge, you could take Roland with you."

"But Papa, Roland can't talk or read the compass if we get lost," I said.

Papa put his chin in his hand and thought hard. "I know!" he said after a moment. "I know who will be a good guide for my two ladies. Dieter! I will ask him if he would like to accompany you. I think his vacation starts next week, and he told me he loves the Zobten Mountain."

"Oh, yes, yes!" I exclaimed joyously.

Papa and I looked at Mother for her reaction. "No,

I don't like that. No," she said.

"But Margarete," Papa said in surprise, "you like that boy. You said so yourself. And Inge—well, she really has become his little sister."

"Maybe," Mother said in a low voice, "but I want *you* with us."

"I'm sorry. That just can't be. You will have to go without me." Papa got up and kissed Mother. "I'll walk over and discuss the trip with Dieter and his parents," he said.

🌿 Chapter Six 🌿

Papa arranged everything, and at the beginning of the following week we left. Mother finally had agreed to the plan and seemed in fine spirits. I was in seventh heaven. A full week, day and night, with Dieter!

The train trip was not long, but, as Mother said, it was "complicated." We had to change trains three times. The last was a small train that had a bell in front, which rang whenever cows were in the meadows near the tracks. It seemed as if the train didn't have the Zobten Mountain in mind as it wound its way slowly through the flat landscape. Sometimes we could see the Zobten ahead of us, rising like a flattened-out, blue ice cream cone on the horizon. At other times the train turned its back to the mountain.

"The train goes out of its way to stop in as many villages as possible," Dieter explained. And at every stop people got on and off the train.

At last we arrived at our destination. "Now comes the hard but fun part," Dieter announced. "From here on we have to climb on foot."

We left our suitcases at the station to be picked up later by porters from the inn, and walked steadily uphill for two hours, stopping often to catch our breath and to look down at the landscape below us. With every step we took the air got fresher and spicier, and suddenly, as we left the woods through which we had walked for the last ten minutes, the mountain inn came into view on a small, flat plateau.

"Hurrah! We've made it," Dieter yelled and let out a yodel. Three yodels answered back.

"Who is that?" I asked.

"The rocks," Dieter said, laughing.

"How can the rocks answer you?" I wanted to know. And Dieter explained what an echo is.

We had to walk for ten more minutes on a winding

path through a blooming meadow before we entered the inn. The host greeted us in the cool, spacious hall. "Your rooms are ready," he said and motioned a young man to show us upstairs.

Mother and I had a corner room with windows in two directions. There was a washstand with a mirror above it, a wardrobe painted with flower garlands, two beds, two chairs and a small table. I had never seen flowers painted on a wardrobe before. I liked them so much I announced I would paint my boring cream-colored wardrobe with flowers as soon as we returned home.

"Of course, of course," Mother said, and smiled absently. I had the feeling she hadn't listened to me. "We should wash off the dust of the trip," Mother said. I didn't see any dust on myself, but she made me wash up anyhow. Mother stretched out on one of the beds while I went from window to window taking in the landscape surrounding the inn.

A gong sounded. "That must be the signal for supper," Mother said, and we went downstairs to the dining room.

Dieter was already sitting at a table. A large vase of meadow flowers stood in the center of it and three colorful, deep bowls were filled with steaming soup. Dieter cut the crusty loaf of dark bread into thick slices and I spread them with butter so deep a yellow as I had never seen before. We all were hungry and ate with pleasure.

I ate very fast and when I came close to the bottom of my bowl, I let out a little cry. "There's a picture!" Hastily, I spooned out everything to the last drop and stared at a picture of a boy and girl dancing, their dainty pointed shoes balancing on a garland of acorns and nuts. It was so pretty I was tempted to lick the dish clean to see the picture even more clearly. Mother and Dieter were watching me, so I decided against it. Then I moved closer to Dieter to see what picture would appear in his bowl. He teased me by eating very slowly, and when he finally emptied the bowl—there was no picture at all. Mother looked on, smiling. She had stopped eating, though her bowl was not empty yet.

"Go on, please," I urged her, but she said she had had enough. "May I finish it then?" I asked.

"Darling, you've eaten a lot," she said. "More than I can get you to eat at home." But she pushed the bowl in front of me anyhow and I quickly finished the soup.

"Oh, how pretty!" I exclaimed, looking at a girl's face smiling up at me.

"Yes," Dieter agreed. "I wish I had had that bowl,

because the girl looks like you, Inge."

I blushed and reached for Dieter's hand under the table. But he put my hand on the table and, still holding it, said, "We have nothing to hide."

I blushed even more and glanced at Mother.

Mother was starting to get up from the table. "We have had a long and strenuous day today," she said, "and we must go to bed early if we want to get up early tomorrow."

"But there's a full moon," Dieter said.

"Yes, yes," I said enthusiastically. "Let's take a long moonlight walk."

Mother could not be persuaded. "We still have to unpack our suitcases," she said. "But we can step outside for just a moment if you wish."

The sky was not dark yet and the moon had not cleared the pine forest at the horizon. Dieter said he would like to take a walk till it got dark. So we said good night, and Mother and I went upstairs to our room. Mother was right, it had been a strenuous day and I fell asleep as soon as I lay down.

When I woke, I thought morning was just breaking. I was only half aware of the pine-spiced mountain air coming through the open window. Slowly I opened my eyes and was surprised to see the full, round moon within arm's reach, just in front of me. I sat up. How could that be? It took me seconds to realize I was seeing the moon's reflection in the mirror on the wall opposite. The whole room was filled with an eerie dim light that gave the furniture an unreal appearance. I reached across the aisle to wake Mother, but my arm was too short. I got out of bed to get closer and carefully felt around in her bed. No Mother! I became frightened. All alone in a strange room in a strange mountain inn.

I switched on the light to see the clock. A quarter to midnight. I opened the door to the hallway. "Mother, Mother," I called softly, not wanting to wake the other guests. In desperation I knocked on Dieter's door. "Dieter, it's Inge," I called in a muffled voice. "Mother's gone. Come, help me look for her." No reply. I knocked again and raised my voice. This time I heard a key being turned in a door across the hall, so I quickly dashed back inside my room. The room was dark. I thought I had left the light on. Then I heard loud snoring. "Who's that?" a harsh voice asked.

Quickly I rushed out and ran to the end of the hall. There in the dimness of a night-light I could see a curtain and I slipped behind it, hitting my leg against something hard. It was pitch dark. I stretched out my hands to feel my way around and reached into something bristly and furry. I suppressed a scream just as I heard a door being opened, then closed somewhere nearby. Then all was quiet again. Only my fast-beating heart drummed in my ears. Dodo taught me to always protect my eyes with one hand, to feel ahead with the other and to take very small steps when walking in the dark. I did just that. Again my hand touched something furry and ticklish and my leg bumped against something sharp. It hurt. I bent down to touch my leg and felt a warm, sticky wetness. Paralyzed, I stood still. When I was sure nobody was in the hall, I parted the curtain, looked for Number 12, our room, and dashed for it. Once inside I felt safe, but terribly worried. Where was Mother? And Dieter!

I turned off the light and walked to the window. Blue! Everything was blue in the moonlight. But clear and sharp just the same. I could see each top spike of the faraway pine trees that formed a black line separating the bright moonlit sky from the moonlight-flooded meadow. The path from the forest to the inn was a winding, glittering ribbon. My heartbeat had calmed down, and suddenly I thought what I had not allowed myself to think—Mother was probably out walking with Dieter! The walk I had wanted to take so much. Fury and sadness welled up

53

within me. But there was nothing I could do about it but wait.

I waited a long time. Once, something came darting out of the darkness of the forest. Soon I saw arms and legs flying around a solid center. With its shadow ahead of it, it resembled a windmill in stormy weather. As it approached the inn I thought I recognized the young man who had shown us to our room on our arrival.

A clock struck midnight. The moon had moved and so had the shadows. Again something loosened itself from the tree line at the end of the meadow. It was huge and it moved very slowly. It must be the cook, I decided. He certainly was big and fat. I left the window to wash the blood off my leg. I had forgotten about it in all the excitement.

When I returned to the window, the wide figure, a bit closer to the inn, split in two. Now there were two figures walking along the path. A few minutes later I could make out a man and a woman, and still later, Dieter and Mother. They stopped just under my window and turned to gaze at the moon. Once Dieter reached for Mother's hand. She pulled it away quickly. When they entered the inn, I closed the window and rushed to my bed, and when Mother came into the room, I pretended to sleep. She put on her nightgown in the dark and let her hair down. Then she walked over to the window and opened it.

A soft whistling of Brahms' "Lullaby" rose up from outside. Mother stood motionless. Her long loose hair caught the moonlight so that her silhouette was brimmed by light. I didn't know how long she stood there. Finally she raised her hand, waved and got into her bed. The whistling continued below. Mother heaved a little sigh and soon fell asleep—long before I did.

 Chapter Seven

The following morning I woke up late. Mother
had left a note for me on the night table:

I will wait for you in the dining room.

I dressed in a hurry, but before going downstairs, I
had to find out what kind of place I had hidden in the
night before. I peeked behind the curtain at the end
of the hall and saw what had scratched, tickled and
scared me: brushes and brooms, cans and buckets. I
should have laughed, but I couldn't. Some of the fear
was still with me.

Mother and Dieter were sitting at our table when I entered the dining room. "We waited for you with breakfast," Mother said, folding her arms around me and giving me a kiss. As if nothing had happened, I thought, and got stiff and rigid in her embrace. I couldn't look Dieter in the face either. How could they betray me so? I sat down while they both looked at me.

"Didn't you sleep well, little sister?" Dieter asked.

"The full moon makes one restless," Mother said with a sigh. "As beautiful as it is, it isn't good for sleeping."

I didn't say a word. I reached for a poppy-seed roll in the bread basket and put butter and honey on it. Mother and Dieter talked about the honey and how different it tasted from the honey at home.

"The bees feed on different blossoms here in the higher altitude," Dieter said.

How smart he is, I thought, and I had to admit to myself I still adored him, in spite of everything.

The days went by quickly. They were filled with hikes interrupted by long rests in sunny meadows or, on hot days, under shady trees. The best part of the day, however, was right after lunch, when Mother took a nap and I had Dieter all to myself for at least an hour. Usually we stayed close to the inn. I would lie on my back in the grass gazing into the sky while

Dieter sat beside me and read aloud. Papa had smuggled a surprise into my suitcase, a book which I had discovered only when unpacking. And now Dieter read it to me. *The Wondrous Travels of Little Nils Holgersson with the Wild Geese* was the title, and it was full of wonderful adventures. Dieter said he liked it, too.

One day, Little Nils Holgersson was in the middle of the most exciting flight when Mother showed up. She couldn't have been away longer than half an hour. She held a book under her arm and said she had not been able to sleep after reading a poem that had moved her *so much*!

"May I read it?" Dieter asked. Mother handed him the book, though she did not let go of it. They both stood there, each with one hand on the book, looking at each other. And, to my disgust, I saw that strange smile come over Mother's face. Finally Mother let go of the book and sat down beside me. Dieter dropped my wonderful *Little Nils Holgersson* and opened Mother's book at the marked page. He started to read aloud in his deep and beautiful voice. I listened—but I could not follow. There was as much talk of longing, loving, waiting and heartbreak as in Emma's kitchen songs. There were tears in Mother's eyes, and Dieter's voice got lower, even trembled at times. At last the poem came to an end. But that

wasn't the end. Mother and Dieter looked at each other again in silence. "I know parts of this poem by heart—in its original language," Dieter said. "It is by Keats. Do you want to hear it in English?"

Mother nodded and Dieter started all over again. Only this time I did not understand a single word. When he had finished, Mother said something to him—also in English! I felt like screaming, but I touched Mother's arm and pleaded, "*Please*, Mother, speak German. I want to understand too."

She only patted my head and went on talking in English, as if I didn't exist. I jumped to my feet and ran into the inn, nearly bumping into the young man who had told me proudly a few days ago that he was a bellhop for the inn. Bellhop! That made me laugh. Now he was standing on a stool with a roll of paper in his hand.

"Say, little lady, can you dance?" he asked cheerfully.

"Dance? Why?" I asked, surprised.

"Well..." he said, unrolling a large poster.

A border of musical notes framed big, brightly colored letters that said:

DANCING—SATURDAY NIGHT
FROM 8 TILL MIDNIGHT

"Well—can you?" he asked.

"Of course I can dance," I replied.

"Well," he said again, "in that case may I have the honor of a dance with you on Saturday?"

I didn't take him seriously, but I nodded anyhow. Then I held down the curled-up bottom edge of the announcement so he could fasten the two upper corners to the wall.

"Step back and tell me how it looks here, between the moose heads," he said.

"Splendid," I said. The two stuffed moose heads with their big antlers had frightened me when I first saw them, but now their spell seemed broken.

"And do you know who the artist of this fine poster is?" the bellhop asked. Without waiting for an answer he tapped his chest with his forefinger and bowed. "I! I am not only a bellhop, I am an artist, too," he announced proudly.

I ran back outdoors. I had to tell Mother and Dieter about the dance.

Mother smiled. "It's a good thing we brought your party dress," she said. Then she told Dieter that I danced well. "But right now," she said, "I want to go back to our room and write a letter to Papa."

"Why don't you write to Dodo, too?" I suggested, hoping to keep her busy for as long as possible.

Dieter and I left Mother and strolled across the meadow. The air smelled of freshly cut grass, and birds crossed back and forth above our heads. One bird swooped down to the top of a pine close by.

"I wish I could be that high up in a tree," I said.

"You can, you know," Dieter said.

I looked at him doubtfully. "How?"

"I know just the right tree," said Dieter. "Come, I'll show you."

We walked around the fenced-in vegetable garden behind the inn, and there, at the edge of the meadow, stood a larch tree, all by itself. Most of the trees on this high plateau were pines with gnarly branches and sharp, prickly needles, but a larch tree has needles that are soft to the touch.

"That's where we will go," Dieter said, pointing to some high branches. "It's higher than the second-floor windows of the inn and we will have a beautiful view."

I was a good climber, but the first branches of the larch were far out of my reach.

Dieter must have noticed my worried look. "Here, I'll lift you up," he said. I reached for the first branch with my hands and Dieter told me to put my feet on his shoulders. After that it was easy. The branches were close together, and in a few minutes I was up very high. Dieter was close behind.

"Wait," he said, "now you must let me go first. I have to test whether the branches will hold us." He climbed slowly and cautiously. "Here," he said, "we'll stop here and look around."

We sat on two different branches and held on to the trunk. The tree swayed slightly in the breeze. It felt delicious. I was so happy I couldn't speak.

"Turn your head to the right," said Dieter, "and look down in the valley. See the church steeple? That's the village where we left the train. You can see the railroad station hanging on the long winding chain of tracks."

"Yes, yes, I see," I said, "and there's a train coming now."

Flat land, out of which the Zobten rose abruptly, spread as far as I could see. Roads meandered in all directions through rectangles and squares of fields and meadows in hues of greens and yellows. It was beautiful to sit there with Dieter, suspended between earth and sky.

"What kind of bird would you like to be?" Dieter asked.

I shrugged.

"I know," he said, "you want to be a lark in a larch tree." And he started to whistle like a lark. After a few seconds he stopped. "Maybe you prefer to be an ordinary sparrow?" Before I could say no, Dieter chirped like a dozen sparrows.

I laughed. "What I would really like to be is a nightingale," I confessed.

"Ah, a nightingale," said Dieter, and he immediately filled the air with the melodious, half-sobbing song of a nightingale.

"I would like to stay here forever," I said, but at that very moment I saw Mother coming out of the inn. How small she looked and how far away from her I felt. She stepped into the meadow and, shielding her eyes with her hand, looked in all directions. She was looking for us, of course.

"Let's stay here a little longer, Dieter," I pleaded.

But Dieter called out to her at the top of his voice and Mother walked toward the tree, her arms spread out. Her white dress set her off against the deep-green grass and her blond, windblown hair shimmered in the sun. It looked like a halo around her head.

"Look, Inge, how pretty our mama looks," Dieter said.

"Come down, my darlings," Mother called. Dieter was already halfway down the tree, but I took my time. With each branch down my heart lost some of its lightness, and by the time I touched the ground, it was heavy. Dieter helped me down from the last branch, but his attention was on Mother.

🌿 Chapter Eight 🌿

On Saturday after lunch the big hall was closed off and the guests were asked to use the back entrance. Supper was served earlier than usual to give everyone time to change for the dance. Mother helped me put on my pink party dress with ruffles and mother-of-pearl buttons up the back. She spent a long time in front of the mirror darkening her eyebrows and powdering her skin. She dabbed pink stuff on her cheeks and perfume behind her ears and on her neck. Holding a small mirror in her hand, she twisted and turned her head like a bird, looking at herself from all sides in the mirror on the wall. When she reached for the powder puff for the hundredth time, I burst out laughing. It was not a good laugh. "It's enough, Mother," I heard myself say in a harsh voice. "It's really enough."

She looked at me, startled. There was silence. After she had fussed some more, she was finally ready to go downstairs. "You can stay up one hour longer tonight," she said, "but then you have to go to bed. You understand?"

I nodded.

We knocked on Dieter's door and he popped out instantly. He had a white handkerchief in his navy-blue jacket, and his curly hair, which always hung loose around his face, was carefully combed. He looked different, but beautiful. He arched his arms for us to put our own arms through, and we went downstairs.

The hall was completely transformed. The furniture had been moved to clear the center; the carpets had been taken out; and colorful streamers floated crisscross from wall to wall. A garland of meadow flowers edged a table that held a huge crystal bowl of punch and big platters of tiny sandwiches and cookies. At the upright piano sat an elderly man, while a younger man stood beside him playing the accordion. Many people from the village had come for the dance, and the air vibrated with music and chatter. We had to zigzag our way between dancing couples to find seats.

The waiter brought two glasses of punch and a pink, bubbling drink for me. Soda with raspberry syrup! We clicked glasses, and Dieter said he was proud to sit between two such pretty ladies. Then he asked me to dance. I had longed for this moment, but now I felt so unsure of myself that I could hardly keep the beat. He will never dance with me again, I thought when the music stopped and we went back to our seats. But when the next dance began, Dieter asked me again. He could have danced with Mother, I told myself, but when he has a choice, he prefers me. And when he asked me for the third dance, my heart was close to bursting. It didn't even matter much that Mother and he talked in English again when we came back to the table.

During the next dance we all sat and sipped our drinks and watched the dancers.

Then the musicians played a waltz and Dieter danced with Mother; I forgave him and looked on. Whenever I could catch a glimpse of them in the swaying crowd, I had to admit to myself they looked nice together. Dieter held Mother away from him and Mother tilted her head from side to side to the rhythm of the music. I must learn how to do that, I thought, and observed Mother carefully. When the waltz ended, the pianist announced an intermission.

The intermission was dreadfully long. I looked at the clock. It was already close to my bedtime. Mother had looked at the clock, too. "In five minutes you'll have to go upstairs, Inge," she said. "Would you like me to put you to bed?"

"Nobody needs to put me to bed," I snapped. "But must I really go already?"

"Maybe I can have a last dance with Inge," Dieter intervened. And since the musicians were just returning, Mother nodded agreement. The dance seemed short. Much too short.

Dieter said he would walk me upstairs, and holding his hand, I took each step as slowly as I could. At our door he kissed me on the cheek and wished me happy dreams. I watched him walk away from me toward the stairs. He turned back once and, seeing me still at the door, said, "Tomorrow Nils Holgersson will fly along the coast of the Baltic Sea. That will be fun."

I entered our room, but did not undress immediately. I stood in front of the mirror, humming a waltz,

70

and practiced tilting my head gracefully from one side to the other.

Then I began to undo the buttons on the back of my dress. It was difficult. I could not reach down far enough. I tried to slip out of my half-unbuttoned dress, but couldn't. Well, that wasn't too bad. It gave me an excuse to go down again and ask Mother for help. Maybe I could even have one more dance with Dieter, now that I knew how to tilt my head gracefully. I stopped on the landing at midstairs to look for Dieter and Mother. When I saw them among the dancers, Dieter was not holding Mother at a distance and Mother did not tilt her head from side to side. She was close to Dieter, with her cheek nearly touching his. They both looked very serious. It must be uncomfortable, I thought, Dieter being so tall and having to bend down while Mother had to dance on her toes. I stood and watched. At the end of the dance, Mother leaned back to look at Dieter and smiled her mysterious smile. Dieter's face remained serious.

The dance ended. When I reached the table, Mother and Dieter were not there. Their two punch glasses stood filled to the brim, so I took a sip and waited. The next dance began, but Dieter and Mother were not among the dancers. I felt thirsty,

so I drank some more punch. It tasted good, though not as good as my soda with raspberry syrup. When the band started to play a new piece, I saw Dieter and Mother dancing cheek to cheek again. I waved, but they didn't notice me and when the dance ended, I saw them walk out the door into the dark night. I didn't want to run after them and look childish, so I decided to go upstairs. But when I tried to stand up, my legs felt as if they were made of rubber. Quickly I sat down again. A lady walking by stared at me. I forced a smile and casually reached for the other full glass. I was hot and thirsty and gulped it down. I waited for the music to resume before I made my way to the stairs, but I had to sit down every few steps and rest. With great effort I finally made it to our room and threw myself on the bed.

I could not sleep. My bed seemed to sway and my stomach seemed to rise within me. After a while I sat up. I had to do *something*. I lit the candle on the night table and stared at it. It gave me comfort. There was a touch of Christmas and a bit of birthdays in its tender light, but I still felt fuzzy. I laid my head back and tried to clear my mind. My head began to hurt; my stomach, too. The candle doubled and tripled in front of my eyes. Beautiful! The whole room was aflame. But I was too tired to watch and fell asleep.

🌿 Chapter Nine 🌿

When I woke up, Dodo was at my bedside. I
closed my eyes again, feeling happy and secure with
her close to me.

"Is the dance over?" I asked.

"Yes, darling," Dodo answered, "it's been over for
a long time—since four days ago."

"Four days?" I cried, and tried to sit up, but could
not. I hurt all over.

"You must stay as quiet as you can," Dodo said.

I looked at my arms—both were in bandages. Only

my hands stuck out at the ends of the white gauze, and they were red. And the room! It was not the room in the mountain inn. It was a small white room with nothing but my bed and a bedside table. "Where am I, Dodo?"

"You are in the hospital, Inge darling," she said. And she told me how Hans, the bellhop, had found me unconscious in the burning room. How he had gotten me out. How I had been brought down to the village in the middle of the night and how Papa had come the next day. And she, too, had come as soon as she could and had spent every moment at my bedside.

"Where are Mother and Papa?" I wanted to know.

"Your Papa had to go home, but only after he was sure you were out of danger," Dodo said. "And Mother is downstairs getting a breath of fresh air. I will call her."

"Not yet," I said and turned my head to the wall. "Where is Dieter?"

"Dieter went home too; but he has written you several letters." Dodo took some envelopes from my bedside table. "Shall I read them to you? Or would you rather read them yourself?"

"Myself," I whispered.

"Then I will call Mother now. She will be so happy

you are awake and can talk to her."

"Not yet," I said. "I want to read Dieter's letters first."

As Dodo handed me the letters, the door opened and in came Mother. Dodo got up and left. Mother sat down, but she didn't say a word. She gently took one of my hands in hers.

"It hurts," I said and pulled it back.

Pain was all over Mother's face. I did not want to watch her cry and turned my face to the wall. In my other hand I still clutched Dieter's letters.

"Have you read them yet?" Mother asked in a trembling voice.

I shook my head.

"Inge, darling—please *speak* to me. I am your mother! And I am happy, so happy, you are all right."

I looked at her. She did not look happy. "You are crying," I said.

"Yes, I am crying because I am thinking what would have happened if I had lost you." After a pause, she added, "It would have been the end of my life, too."

"It would not!" I said. "You have Papa and you have Dodo... *and* Dieter."

"Yes," Mother said, "and they are all dear to me. All for different reasons. But not one of them could ever take your place. *You* I love most."

I did not like the outburst of tears that followed, so I closed my eyes and turned to the wall, hoping Mother would leave me alone. After a while Mother bent over and kissed me on the forehead and went to the door. But she didn't leave. She turned back to sit beside my bed again. I could hear her muffled voice under suppressed sobs. "Darling, darling, I hope you — will forgive me. I hope one day you will understand. I was lonely and Dieter's admiration meant a lot to me. And I was sure you were happy with your new big brother too."

"I would have been if..." I murmured, and stopped.

"If what?"

"If you hadn't taken him away from me all the time."

"But darling, you misunderstand. I was happy to see how much you liked each other."

I turned my face to her and opened my eyes. She looked exhausted and worried. Impulsively I stretched out my hand toward her. She smiled. "I don't want to hurt you again by touching," she said. "I'll blow a little butterfly kiss." And Mother bent forward and blew on my hand. It felt good and I smiled back. We looked at each other for a long time.

Finally Mother said, "I'll go and phone Papa now and tell him how well you are—and if he needs me, I might go home now and leave you here with Dodo."

I nodded and Mother left the room.

Dodo returned a few minutes later. "Thank goodness, your mother is herself again," she said. "The past three days I didn't know how to comfort her."

An hour later Mother came back. "I'm sorry, I must go home now, Inge," she said. "Papa does need me. But Dodo will stay with you, and very soon we will all be together again—and happy. I just talked to the doctor, and he said you will be able to come home in a few days."

She kissed me and stroked my cheek, then said good-bye to Dodo and left.

"Would you like to read Dieter's letters now?" Dodo asked. She opened them for me. "I think I will go for a breath of fresh air myself," she said, and left the room.

I read the letters in the order of their dates. The first one, written before Dieter left the inn, was full of things remembered; how nice it was to dance with me and how sad that an evening so full of joy should have ended with having to bring me unconscious down to the village hospital. In the next letter Dieter told me he had gone to our secret spot and talked

with Roland. "Guess what we talked about?" Dieter wrote. "About you, of course, our princess." The third envelope was very fat. A small silken handkerchief was inside; it had a delicate border of forget-me-nots along the edges. Dieter told me he often looked at the brown eyes staring up at him from the otherwise still-white page of his drawing pad, and that he was looking forward to adding blond hair, rosy cheeks and a smiling mouth to them very soon.

I kissed each page before I put it back in its envelope.

Now only one letter was left. Should I leave it for the next day and read the others again? No, a new letter will arrive, I told myself, and I started to read:

Dear Inge-sister,

Today I have to tell you something that makes me sad and glad. Yesterday I received the news that I have been accepted as an apprentice in a large and famous art studio in Berlin. I will have to leave tomorrow. I am sad, very sad, that I will not be here when you come home. I will miss you dearly, and I will also miss your mother. I have learned so much from her. She has added new poets and new painters to my life. Through her eyes I have learned to see more beauty. And in long talks with her I found

comfort and order in a world that sometimes bewil-
dered me. I am glad you have each other. You will not
feel as lonely as I will feel so far away from you both.
But when I do, the thought of you and your mother
will comfort me. I will not forget you. I will write
when I am settled, and you must write, too.

Good-bye,
Your Dieter-brother

*   *   *

A few days later my thick bandages were ex-
changed for very light ones, and the day after that we
left for home. On the long train ride I talked to Dodo
about Dieter for the first time. I told her how we had
met at the fence. How he had left little presents for
me there. How he could jump over the brook—with
me in his arms. How he was full of tricks, all for me. I
told her what a fine artist he was and, fighting back
my tears, that now he was going away to Berlin.

Dodo did not say a word while I spoke. She just
nodded her head and listened.

"What shall I do, Dodo? I love him so, but he cares
more for Mother than for me."

"I am not sure that is true, though they do have a
lot in common," Dodo said. "Things you do not
understand yet."

"What things?" I asked. "I understand moonlight

walks and I understand books. I can dance, too—and gracefully. I can even tilt my head back and forth."

"Yes, darling, I know. But there are other things that grown-ups share. You will find out later."

"I want to know *now*," I insisted.

But Dodo shook her head gently and said, "I can't explain, Inge. You just must believe me."

Sadness welled up inside me. For the first time in my life Dodo could not help me. What should I do? Should I tell her about their midnight return from the moonlight walk? Their speaking English so I would not understand? Their dancing cheek to cheek? And Mother's smile and the photo in the jewelry box? Did Dodo know about all that? I wanted to blurt it all out, but something kept me from doing so. For as long as I could remember I had always told Dodo everything. But now I kept silent. I felt there were things that I could not put into words.

🌿 Chapter Ten 🌿

It was late afternoon when Papa and Mother met us at the railroad station. I was tired, but Papa and Mother looked so happy and laughed so much it made me feel good. Emma and Roland met us at the garden gate. Roland greeted me with barks and licks, and Emma whispered into my ear, "I have a new fiancé *and* a new record—I'll play it for you tomorrow."

Roland kept close to my side. "He has missed you a lot," Papa said. "He sat at the door of your bedroom every night and howled."

For supper we had my favorite sausages, and for dessert, raspberries with whipped cream.

Before going to bed I walked through the garden. I didn't want to go to my secret place, but I was drawn to it. I parted the branches and entered. My foot hit a stone, and I bent down to pick it up. It was an ordinary gray fieldstone of nearly perfect oval shape. On the raised side a fine line was scratched into the stone. It was a face. A face that looked like mine. I turned the stone over. On its flat bottom were scratched four lines.

A PAPERWEIGHT FOR INGE
TO WEIGH DOWN THE LETTERS
SHE WILL RECEIVE
FROM HER DIETER-BROTHER

I pressed the cool stone to my cheek and slowly walked back to the house. Halfway there I met Mother. I could not hide the stone, and she took it in her hands to look at.

She stroked it and said, "Yes, Inge, we both have lost a friend we badly needed. For you, Dieter was a brother to shorten long and lonely summer days after Erika died, and for me, he was a friend with whom I could share poems and books and talk about music and art when poor Papa had to spend so much time at his work."

84

I nodded and reached for Mother's hand. She knelt down, put her arms around me and held me tight. I buried my head in her shoulder and kissed her neck. From the house Papa called for Mother, but she did not answer. She took my head between her hands, looked deep into my eyes and smiled.

"I have some plans for us," she said. "The two of us will go for walks, take our drawing pads and draw meadows and trees—whatever we see. Let's start with the pond tomorrow."

"And put mermaids in it?" I interrupted.

"Put mermaids in it if we see some," Mother agreed, laughing.

"And if we make a very good picture, we will send it to Dieter," I said.

Papa called again. We got up and went inside. Mother brought me to bed, kissed me good night and, leaving the door ajar, went downstairs. Then, as she so often did at night, Mother played the piano, and music drifted up to my room.

I closed my eyes, and soon I was walking hand in hand with Dieter through dream-meadows, fields and woods.